For Dorothee

First published in the United States, Great Britain, Canada,
Australia, and New Zealand in 1994 by North-South Books,
an imprint of Nord-Süd Verlag AG, Gossau Zürich, Switzerland.

First published in Switzerland under the title *Der echte Nikolaus bin ich!*

Distributed in the United States by North-South Books Inc., New York.

Library of Congress Cataloging-in-Publication Data is available.
A CIP catalogue record for this book is available from The British Library.
ISBN 1-55858-318-1 (trade binding)
ISBN 1-55858-319-X (library binding)

1 3 5 7 9 10 8 6 4 2

Printed in Belgium

I'm the Real Santa Claus!

By Ingrid Ostheeren
Illustrated by
Christa Unzner

Translated by
Rosemary Lanning

North-South Books
NEW YORK / LONDON

It was Christmas Eve. Santa Claus's reindeer were harnessed to his sleigh, and the elves had loaded sackfuls of presents. Now all that remained for Santa to do was put on his warmest clothes and check his list to see which children had been good.

Then, with a merry laugh, he flew away.

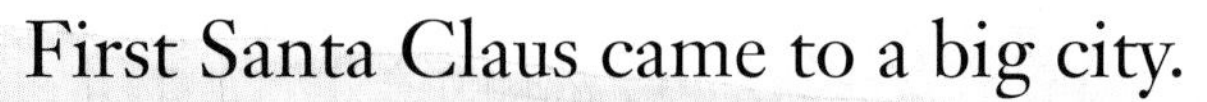

First Santa Claus came to a big city.

"Oh, goodness," he said to himself. "I think I've arrived much too early! I've never seen the city so crowded."

The streets were bustling with Christmas shoppers, so it was hard for Santa to find a place to set down his sleigh. When at last he did, a stern voice from behind him said, "You can't park here. Didn't you see the sign?"

"But I'm Santa Claus," he protested.

"That's what they all say," said the policeman, but then he stopped writing out the parking ticket. "Listen," he said, "I know what it's like. I was Santa Claus myself once, at the children's hospital. All the same, don't let me catch you again or I'll have to give you a parking ticket."

Santa was confused by what the policeman had said. "Surely there's only one Santa Claus," he thought as he strode down the street, "and that's me."

But everywhere he looked he saw more and more people dressed just like him. One of them, coming the other way, waved at him and shouted, "I see we rented our costumes from the same place! You can tell by the nose. Very lifelike, isn't it!"

Outside a department store stood yet another Santa Claus, a large one, shouting and ringing a bell.

"Hey, you," he said when he saw the real Santa Claus. "Go and find somewhere else to stand. This is my territory."

Just then a woman marched out of the store, pulling a little girl behind her. Santa Claus had a beautiful doll in his hand, but before he could give it to the little girl, her mother dragged her away.

"Never take presents from strangers!" she snapped.

"Oh please!" cried the little girl. "It is Christmas!"

Santa Claus went into the next building. He knew two boys lived there who hadn't been very good this year. Since he couldn't deliver his presents until everyone was asleep, he decided to speak to them seriously.

Suddenly a tall, thin Santa Claus came rushing down the stairs. "Hello," he said. "Are you looking for Thomas and Martin? I've just delivered some toys to them."

"But those boys haven't been at all good," said Santa Claus.

"It's not my job to tell them that," said the young man. "The toy shop just hires me to make deliveries."

Santa went sadly back to his sleigh. It seemed as if anyone could be Santa Claus now. All a person had to do was wear a costume.

"No one needs me," he thought. "I might as well go home."

Suddenly, three Santas came running out of a bank on the opposite side of the road. One threw a shopping bag straight at him. "Meet us in the forest at midnight!" he shouted as he ran away.

As Santa Claus looked in the bag, police cars came roaring round the corner, their sirens wailing. The bag was stuffed full of money. Those Santas had just robbed a bank! Shaking his head, Santa Claus tossed the bag on his sleigh.

Two policemen ran up. "Stop! Don't move!" shouted one of them. "You're under arrest."

"No, let him go," said the other. "I've seen him before. He's..." The policeman lowered his voice to a whisper, but Santa Claus could still hear what he said: "...the old fellow's not quite right in the head. He thinks he's the *real* Santa Claus." Then he shouted to Santa, "The big red nose, that's real, eh?"

"Of course," said Santa Claus indignantly. He was very proud of his nose.

"See what I mean," the policeman whispered. "He's not one of the robbers. Let's go."

Santa Claus was cold, tired, and miserable.

As he stood in the snow, he saw a woman outside her house, calling her cat. "Hello, Santa Claus!" she said cheerfully.

"You know I'm the *real* Santa Claus, don't you?" he asked.

"Of course," she said, "and I've always wanted to meet you. Why don't you come inside and warm up?"

"The grown-ups don't seem to know who I am," said Santa Claus sadly as the woman poured him a cup of tea.

"That's because they've stopped believing in you," she said. "But the children still love you."

"And do they still like presents?" said Santa Claus.

"Of course," said the woman. "Children love to get presents."

Santa Claus looked out of the window. "It's getting very dark," he said. "I think I'd best be on my way. I musn't let the children down."

Santa Claus thanked the woman for her kindness. Then, just as he was about to drive away, he remembered the bag of money.

"What happens to stolen money?" he asked. The woman looked at him in horror.

"I just heard about a bank robbery on the radio," she said. "That wasn't you, was it?"

Santa Claus told her how the robbers had thrown the money at him. He gave her the bag, and she promised to take it to the police.

"There will be a reward for that," she said.

"Please use it to buy a present for yourself and the cat," said Santa Claus.

All night long Santa hurried from house to house. He piled the big presents under the Christmas trees and stuffed the small ones in the stockings hung from mantelpieces.

Just as he was getting ready to go back home, he saw a little girl waving to him from a window. She was clutching the teddy bear he had left for her.

"I've stayed up all night to see you," she called. "My brother says there is no Santa Claus, but I just *knew* you were real!"